Secrets in the Attic
Copyright © 2022 by Nelibeth Plaza

Published in the United States of America

ISBN   Paperback: 978-1-958030-33-2
ISBN   eBook: 978-1-958030-34-9

All rights reserved. No part of this publication may be reproduced, stored in a retrieval system or transmitted in any way by any means, electronic, mechanical, photocopy, recording or otherwise without the prior permission of the author except as provided by USA copyright law.

The opinions expressed by the author are not necessarily those of ReadersMagnet, LLC.

ReadersMagnet, LLC
10620 Treena Street, Suite 230 | San Diego, California, 92131 USA
1.619. 354. 2643 | www.readersmagnet.com

Book design copyright © 2022 by ReadersMagnet, LLC. All rights reserved.

Cover design by Kent Chu
Interior design by Ched Celiz

Acknowledgments

I like to thank my daughter Rebekkah, for her time and patience in the revision and constructive feedback.

I want to take this opportunity to thank my three grandchildren: Mya, Charlie, and Jacob, God has truly blessed me.

I am delighted and impressed by each of their differences, talents and creativity.

I am thankful and grateful that I have been given, the opportunity to observe my grandchildren, and to use some of their character traits in my stories.

In addition, I like to thank Jessi Russell, for taking the time for her suggestions and ideas.

SECRETS IN THE ATTIC

Nelibeth Plaza

ReadersMagnet, LLC

**Moral:
Kindness and respect for all
Regardless of differences**

It was winter and Christmas Day had passed. Papa climbed a step ladder to remove the Christmas wreath and lights from the window. Mama put Christmas ornaments and decorations into storage boxes. Mya, Charlie and Jacob helped Mama with the boxes. They carried the boxes up the spiral staircase into the attic, which Papa had made into a beautiful playroom.

In the attic was a storage space. It was dark and gloomy unlike the rest of the attic, which was full of color and light. It was furnished with child-sized furniture, like the bean bags the children sat on while reading. On the oak floor lay a lime green area rug where they played board games, and a table with four chairs for homework time.

Most of all, Charlie and Jacob loved sitting on the gray cushioned chairs while playing video games on the flat screened TV mounted on the wall.

Charlie handed a box of Christmas decorations to Papa and said, "Papa, these are the last of the boxes. We're almost done."

"Oh, wonderful! I am so hungry. I can smell the garlic and herb chicken roasting in the oven, and the sweet potatoes too," Papa said. His mouth watered just talking about dinner. He piled the last boxes on a shelf in the storage area.

"Well, Papa, until next Christmas," Charlie said, and gave a sigh of relief.

Mama Rebekkah sent the children to wash up before setting the table for supper. Mya set the placemats and then the plates. Jacob set the napkins and silverware. Charlie placed the glasses and filled them up with milk. Papa took the steaming hot roasted chicken out of the oven, and Mama took out the sweet potatoes and buttery corn on the cob. Everyone took their seats at the table, held hands and Papa said grace.

After dinner, the children went to the playroom in the attic while Mama and Papa cleaned the kitchen. The children played with their new Christmas gifts. Mya painted on the easel and Charlie played a video game. Jacob played with a remote controlled pick-up truck. It was bright red, the doors opened, the headlights blinked, and the horn beeped. Jacob moved the controller making the truck go forward and backward. He made it zoom passed the play area and into the storage area.

The truck got stuck behind some boxes. Jacob had a hard time finding the truck. It was too dark, so he got a flashlight. As he searched, he spotted a quick moving shadow, but saw nothing. He found the truck and continued playing.

A few days later, Charlie asked Jacob, "Who ate my leftover slice of pepperoni pizza?"

Jacob replied, "I didn't."

"That's funny because Mya doesn't like leftover pizza, and Mama and Papa never eat from the refrigerator in the attic," Charlie said.

Charlie and Jacob were speechless wondering about the mysteriously disappearing slice of pizza.

One Saturday afternoon, the children were sitting on bean bags reading books. Mya wanted a snack. She skipped into the mini kitchen, but quickly ran back to her brothers. Her face was beet-red, and her hands were in tight fists on her hips. She said, "Hey, which one of you ate my brownie with all the nuts on top?"

Charlie and Jacob said at the same time, "Not me!"

Charlie stood up and said, "Something fishy is going on here. Three days ago my slice of pepperoni pizza went missing too."

Jacob was silent, but he had an idea of who was behind the missing food - the neighborhood squirrel family; Pepito, Isabella, Margarita, and Ponchito.

Last year, on Christmas Eve, they snuck into their house and ate Mama's homemade chocolate chip cookies.

Mya said, "I have a feeling that it is a squirrel. We should tell Papa. He will know how to safely set a trap."

"No, let's keep this a secret. I will get to the bottom of this," Charlie said.

They all agreed and pinky promised to keep the secret.

A week later, Jacob was playing in the attic with his red pick-up truck. It got stuck again in the storage area. He grabbed the flashlight. He shined the light, but did not see the truck. Instead he saw a teeny tiny shadow like the last time. He followed the shadow to a back wall. The shadow was a creature and it was trapped with nowhere else to hide.

Jacob shined the light on the creature and said, "It is you, Ponchito." Jacob was excited and curious. He asked, "What are you doing in the attic? Where are your parents, Pepito and Isabella? Where is your sister, Margarita? Are you all living in the attic?"

All Ponchito could do was tremble.

"Hey, I'm sorry," Jacob said. "I didn't mean to scare you. Let me introduce myself properly. My name is Jacob."

Ponchito stood frozen like a popsicle.

"You stay right here. I'll be right back with a surprise," Jacob said, and he ran into the kitchen, opened the refrigerator, and grabbed a plate of apple slices.

Jacob whispered, "Ponchito, Ponchito, where are you? I have something yummy for your tummy."

Finally, Ponchito's teeny tiny head popped up from behind a storage box.

"Don't be afraid. I brought you a sweet treat," Jacob said.

Ponchito grabbed an apple slice from Jacob's hand, and ate apple slices until they were all gone.

"I was so hungry. I appreciate the apple. It was amazingly delicious. I'm tired of nuts. I really love homemade cooked meals. I am the one eating your food," Ponchito confessed.

Jacob said, "So you're the one behind the disappearing pizza and brownie."

"Yes, it was me. My parents have no idea that I sneak out at night to eat food from the attic. They think I'm asleep," Ponchito said. "My family lives in a tree near your yard. During the day, my parents gather nuts and my sister and I play racing to the top of the tree. At night, we gather inside the tree. My home is dry and warm made up of twigs, grass, soft feathers, and other things we find in the environment."

"Wow, that sounds fun and comfy," Jacob said.

"Yes, at night, we cuddle to stay warm, but sometimes I want to explore. I wiggle myself from under the blanket of leaves after everyone is asleep. My parents are suspicious of humans. They would be furious if they knew I was talking with you," Ponchito said.

It was getting late, and Mama Rebekkah called to the children, "Bedtime."

Ponchito shivered. He said, "It's a really cold night, and has been snowing all day." He did not want to leave, but knew he had to.

Jacob asked, "Will I see you again?"

"Sure! I can come back tomorrow and meet you right here."

The following evening, after supper, Jacob placed leftover hamburger and french fries inside a cloth napkin. As usual, the children went up the spiral staircase leading to the attic while their parents cleaned up the dinner dishes.

Jacob grabbed the flashlight and ran into the storage area. He kneeled down on the oak floor, and whispered, "Ponchito, Ponchito, where are you? I have something delicious for you."

Ponchito poked out his little head, and said, "Here I am. Something smells amazing."

Jacob handed the food and Ponchito ate all of it. Ponchito's full and round belly popped out of his tiny pants. Jacob chuckled.

Jacob showed his red pick-up truck to Ponchito, and he climbed inside for a quick ride. Charlie walked over toward Jacob and noticed the squirrel inside of the truck. Ponchito panicked and jumped out and ran. He slipped and slid across the wooden floor, but was able to escape into the storage area. He hid behind a stack of boxes.

Jacob grabbed Charlie's hand and pleaded, "Please, Charlie, you can't tell Papa. He will set a trap to capture Ponchito, but he is my new best friend."

Jacob's tears began rolling down his round red cheeks. Charlie looked at his brother's sad and teary eyes. He didn't have the heart to break up this new friendship, so he reassured Jacob that he would keep his secret. They made a pinky promise.

Three days passed and Ponchito did not visit. The children sat reading books when all of a sudden, Jacob felt a gentle tug at the bottom of his pants. It was Ponchito. Mya screamed at the sight of a squirrel in the playroom. Charlie tried to muffle her scream by placing his hand in front of her mouth.

Ponchito shivered. Jacob introduced Ponchito to Charlie and Mya, and said, "This is my best friend." Charlie smiled and Mya said, "He is cute."

Mama entered the attic to announce that it was past their bedtime. Ponchito had just left the attic after playing a game with the children.

The temperature had dropped while Ponchito was in the attic. Snow was falling. The winds picked up blowing icy air and snow in all directions. Ponchito could not see the trees as he traveled back home to his tree. He only saw a wall of blowing snow. Holding tight onto tree branches, Ponchito was able to make it home.

The sky looked menacing. It was moonless and starless - just darkness. The wind howled eerily. Cars buried under snow took the shape of large creatures sleeping or waiting in the dark.

A week later, Ponchito appeared in the attic with his sister, Margarita. Mya was happy because now she had a new friend. Mya and Margarita played dress-up using Mya's collection of doll clothing. Margarita tried on dresses, sweaters, scarves, hats, and shoes. They all fit her perfectly. Her favorite was the purple ballerina outfit with the rainbow tutu. After dress-up, they sat for a tea party and ate strawberry shortcake cookies.

Charlie and Jacob help Ponchito get into the red pick-up truck. The headlights were on, and Ponchito beeped the horn.

Mama Rebekkah was heard climbing the spiral staircase. "Quick, hide behind the bean bags," Charlie urged Ponchito.

"Children, the mayor just announced on TV that all schools will be closed due to the blizzard," Mama said.

The children jumped up and down yelling, "Hooray. Yippee. Woohoo. We have a snow day."

Later that evening, Margarita trembled. Her eyes were swollen and filled with tears. Ponchito's teeny tiny legs were shaking like a leaf. They feared the worse hearing the loud sound of cracking and falling trees.

An uncomfortable and tense stillness filled the air. Ponchito and Margarita looked out of the attic window. They could see the tree that had fallen. It was their home. They would also discover that they had lost their parents, and were orphans. Unfortunately, the blizzard was destructive causing damages and losses all over the city.

Mya, Charlie and Jacob were very sad and comforted their friends. "You can stay with us," Jacob said.

"Great idea, Jacob," Charlie affirmed. "Yes, it would be great having you both live with us."

"In fact, I will make beds right now," Mya said.

Margarita sniffled and wiped away tears, and said, "Mya, you are my best friend. I appreciate your kindness." She grabbed Mya's pinky finger, and they ran off together to make the two new beds.

The following day, the children woke up to the sound of chainsaws. They ran to the window and saw emergency workers trying to get the electricity back on again for the city. They had on white hard hats, and were cutting tree branches and removing them from the backyard. Ponchito and Margarita were still asleep in their new beds in the attic.

Mya asked, "How are we going to tell Mama and Papa?"

Charlie replied, "We have to tell them the truth."

"We have to adopt them into our family," Jacob insisted.

The children set the table for breakfast. Once everyone was sitting and began eating pancakes and sausages, Charlie said, "Papa, we have something to tell you and Mama. We have been keeping secrets in the attic."

Papa leaned forward giving his full attention.

Charlie continued, "Ponchito and Margarita, the two squirrel kids who ate Mama's cookies last Christmas Eve, have been visiting us in the attic for weeks now."

"We are great friends, Papa," Mya added. "Margarita is terrific. We play dress-up and have fabulous tea parties."

"I cannot imagine going to the attic and not seeing Ponchito. He is always patiently waiting for a ride in my truck," Jacob said.

Charlie explained to Mama and Papa that Ponchito and Margarita were orphans. They needed a family to adopt them.

Papa took a deep breath and a sip of coffee. There was a long silence and Papa had a concerned look on his face. Finally, he said, "Take some breakfast up to your guests in the attic. Mama and I need to have a talk about this adoption."

After some time, Mama and Papa walked up the spiral staircase and entered the playroom. Jacob introduced Ponchito, and Mya introduced Margarita. Papa said, "I am sorry for your loss, Ponchito and Margarita." Then Mama made the announcement, "Welcome to our family."

The children were ecstatic, jumping up and down. Everyone was hugging and kissing one another. Ponchito and Margarita were adopted. Life was wonderful from that moment on.

A year later, Mama was baking delicious chocolate chip cookies for Santa. Papa came home with the most beautiful Christmas tree. Mya, Charlie, Jacob, Ponchito and Margarita all ran up the spiral staircase to the attic. They ran passed the toys and games and into the storage area. They each grabbed a box of Christmas ornaments and decorations.

This Christmas would be extra special. Papa closed the hole that Ponchito and Margarita used to enter the attic. When Ponchito saw the sealed hole, he remembered sneaking in and eating Charlie's slice of pizza and Mya's brownie. He said to himself, *what an amazing and extraordinary life we all have!*

The End

10620 Treena Street, Suite 230

San Diego, California,

CA 92131 USA

www.readersmagnet.com

1.619.354.2643

Copyright 2022 All Rights Reserved

www.ingramcontent.com/pod-product-compliance
Lightning Source LLC
LaVergne TN
LVHW070218080526
838202LV00067B/6849